THIS WALKER BOOK
BELONGS TO:

....
....

To the Underwoods

First published 1989 by Walker Books Ltd
87 Vauxhall Walk, London SE11 5HJ

This edition published 2008

2 4 6 8 10 9 7 5 3 1

© 1989, 2008 Charlotte Voake

The right of Charlotte Voake to be identified
as author/illustrator of this work has been asserted by her in
accordance with the Copyright, Designs and Patents Act 1988

This book has been handlettered by Charlotte Voake.

Printed in China

British Library Cataloguing in Publication Data: a catalogue
record for this book is available from the British Library

ISBN 978-1-4063-1271-3

www.walkerbooks.co.uk

MRS GOOSE'S BABY

Charlotte Voake

WALKER BOOKS

AND SUBSIDIARIES

LONDON · BOSTON · SYDNEY · AUCKLAND

One day Mrs Goose found an egg

and made a lovely nest to put it in.

Mrs Goose sat on the egg

to keep it safe and warm.

Soon the egg started to crack open.

The little bird inside was
pecking at the shell.

Mrs Goose's baby was very very small
and fluffy and yellow.

Mrs Goose took her baby out
to eat some grass.

But her baby didn't want to eat grass.
She ran off to look for
something different.

Mrs Goose took her naughty baby
to the pond.
The water looked cold and grey.

Poor Mrs Goose!
Her baby would not swim!

 The baby grew

and grew

and grew.

Mrs Goose's feathers were smooth and white.

Mrs Goose's baby had untidy brown feathers.

Mrs Goose had large webbed feet. Her baby had little pointed toes.

The baby followed Mrs Goose everywhere,
and cuddled up to her at night.

Mrs Goose guarded her baby
from strangers.

Mrs Goose's baby never did
eat much grass.

HONK!

The baby never did go swimming
in the pond.

And everyone except Mrs Goose knew why.

Mrs Goose's baby was a

CHICKEN!

Charlotte Voake

The work of Charlotte Voake is renowned throughout the world for its gentle wit, quiet observation, airy exuberance, and charm. Winner of the **Smarties Book Prize** for *Ginger*, Charlotte says of her work, *"I just draw with ink, over and over again – until I think, 'Aha, that's how it should be!'"*

ISBN 978-1-4063-1269-0

ISBN 978-1-4063-1270-6

ISBN 978-1-4063-1271-3

ISBN 978-1-4063-1272-0

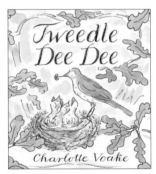

ISBN 978-1-4063-0714-6

ISBN 978-1-4063-0523-4

ISBN 978-0-7445-8958-0

ISBN 978-1-4063-1405-2

Available from all good bookstores

www.walkerbooks.co.uk